D1496639

OBEE AND THE GREAT BANK HEIST

Written by Shirley Tjernagel

Illustrated by Dan Drewes

AuthorHouse™
1663 Liberty Drive
Bloomington, IN 47403
www.authorhouse.com
Phone: 1-800-839-8640

First published by AuthorHouse 6/10/2011

ISBN: 978-1-4634-1913-4 (sc)

Library of Congress Control Number: 2011909912

Printed in the United States of America

This book is printed on acid-free paper.

authorHOUSE®

Somebody has got to pinch me! I couldn't believe my eyes! If you know Obee then you already know that somehow, when Obee's around, things happen that can't be explained. Okay, so I'll tell you what happened and I'll let you figure it out...

Dean, Michelle, and I were sitting on the front porch and Obee was laying near us on the floor of the porch taking a nap. Suddenly, Obee jumped up and he looked to the north and soon it became clear as to what startled him. With his big ears, Obee hears so much more so much sooner than I do.

Up the road dust was flying and a siren was blasting. In the distance we could barely see two cars, one behind the other, speeding down our dusty gravel road.

Obee stuck his head between the posts of the railing on the porch to get a better view as we looked in disbelief on the chase happening before us. All of a sudden, squeezing himself between the railings, Obee jumps off the porch.

We called for him to come back but he ran down through the pasture beside the road and then was out of sight. As it turned out, it was the Sheriff chasing another car but they both passed our place and everything calmed down.

Here's were it gets weird. We're watching the 6 o'clock news and they said that there had been a bank robbery in town and that the authorities were searching for the robbers and sure enough it was the car that had raced by our house that day the Sheriff was chasing them.

The next morning everything was quiet as it usually is on Saturday mornings. Dean and I walked out to have a cup of coffee on the back porch. Sitting in the morning's cool air I notice Obee, Anna (our house cat), and Autumn (our mouser cat that lives outside) were all coming out of the field where Obee had went in the day before. Without noticing we were watching them, they sat at the edge of the field and then they turned around and went back into the tall weeds.

I am a little nosy myself so I snuck around quietly to the field and through the weeds where I watched the strangest thing. Obee was covering something with his nose. Anna was watching from one direction and Autumn from the other. I stood there rubbing my eyes, thinking surely I must be dreaming. Autumn suddenly let out a screeching ear-piercing meow.

I turned to look at her and she had her claws out as a squirrel came near to see what was going on. As the squirrel came nearer Autumn swatted at him and off he darted in the other direction. I realized then that her and Anna were on guard for what ever Obee had buried. When I got back to the house I told Dean and Michelle what I had seen.

For three days I watched Autumn, Anna, and Obee go to the field and back. I couldn't take it any more. With spade in hand, I walked to the very spot where fresh dirt could be seen in the weeds. I looked around, I don't know what for but it was almost spooky. As I bent down I began to dig. The hole was bigger than I thought . I realized how hard those three must have worked to pull this off. What wonderful team work! Then punch, yeah that's what it sounded and felt like, like I'd punched a bag of something...I don't know what. I pulled the bag from the remaining dirt and took it back inside. It was a bag of money! "Oh, my Jesus!", I said. I took the bag to show Dean and Michelle.

Obee, Anna, and Autumn sat in front of us like as though their hearts were broken. Maybe Obee thought he'd plant the bag of money and he'd grow a money tree, we all know that can't happen.

Well, as the story goes, we called the Sheriff and he came to see us. He informed us that it was the money the robbers had heisted from the bank and during the chase they must have threw the bag out into the ditch and that's where Obee had found it.

We told the Sheriff how our pets had hid it and protected it and he, in turn, notified the bank that had gotten robbed.

The bank invited Obee, Anna, and Autumn up to there place of business with Dean, Michelle, and myself. They gave Obee a big bag of doggie bones and Anna and Autumn each a can of sardines. The newspaper photographer was there and the next day he had all three animals on the front page. Our three heroes never seemed so pleased.

~The End~

CPSIA information can be obtained
at www.ICGtesting.com
Printed in the USA
LVRC01n2234280918
591752LV00001B/12

*9 7 8 1 4 6 3 4 1 9 1 3 4 *